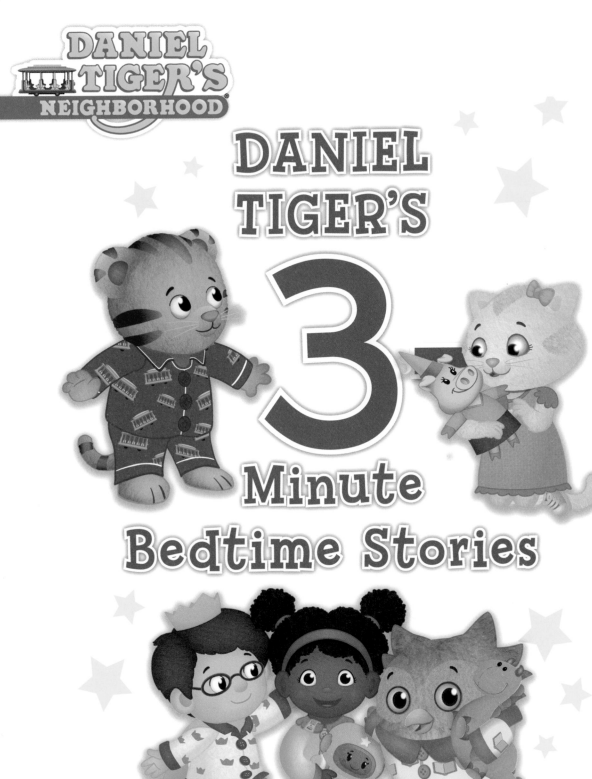

DANIEL TIGER'S NEIGHBORHOOD

DANIEL TIGER'S 3-Minute Bedtime Stories

Simon Spotlight

New York   London   Toronto   Sydney   New Delhi

SIMON SPOTLIGHT

An imprint of Simon & Schuster Children's Publishing Division

1230 Avenue of the Americas, New York, New York 10020

This Simon Spotlight edition October 2018

Meet the Neighbors, Friends Are the Best!, and *Snowflake Day!* © 2014 The Fred Rogers Company

How Is Daniel Feeling?, Daniel's Sweet Trip to the Bakery, Big Brother Daniel, and *What's Special at Night?* © 2015 The Fred Rogers Company

A Duckling for Daniel and *You're Still You!* © 2016 The Fred Rogers Company

Daniel Loves Fall!, Going to See Grandpere, and *King Daniel the Kind* © 2017 The Fred Rogers Company

Meet the Neighbors! by Natalie Shaw

Friends Are the Best! by Maggie Testa, poses and layouts by Jason Fruchter

How Is Daniel Feeling? adapted by Maggie Testa, poses and layouts by Jason Fruchter

Daniel's Sweet Trip to the Bakery adapted by Maggie Testa, based on the screenplay "I Love You, Mom" written by Angela C. Santomero, poses and layouts by Jason Fruchter

Big Brother Daniel by Angela C. Santomero, poses and layouts by Jason Fruchter

A Duckling for Daniel adapted by Angela C. Santomero, based on the episode "Daniel Tiger Waits for Show and Tell" written by Angela C. Santomero, poses and layouts by Jason Fruchter

You're Still You! adapted by Maggie Testa, based on the episode "No Red Sweater for Daniel" written by Dan Yaccarino and "Teacher Harriet's New Hairdo" written by Becky Friedman, poses and layouts by Jason Fruchter

King Daniel the Kind adapted by Angela C. Santomero, based on the screenplay written by Becky Friedman and Angela C. Santomero, poses and layouts by Jason Fruchter

Going to See Grandpere adapted by Daphne Pendergrass, poses and layouts by Jason Fruchter

Daniel Loves Fall! adapted by Natalie Shaw, based on the screenplay written by Jill Cozza-Turner, poses and layouts by Jason Fruchter

Snowflake Day! adapted by Becky Friedman, based on the screenplay written by Angela C. Santomero and Becky Friedman, poses and layouts by Jason Fruchter

What's Special at Night? adapted by Daphne Pendergrass, based on the screenplay "Nighttime in the Neighborhood" written by Becky Friedman, poses and layouts by Jason Fruchter

All rights reserved, including the right of reproduction in whole or in part in any form.

SIMON SPOTLIGHT and colophon are registered trademarks of Simon & Schuster, Inc.

For information about special discounts for bulk purchases, please contact Simon & Schuster Special Sales at 1-866-506-1949 or business@simonandschuster.com.

Manufactured in China 1018 SCP

10 9 8 7 6 5 4 3 2 1

ISBN 978-1-5344-2859-1

ISBN 978-1-5344-2860-7 (eBook)

ISBN 978-1-5344-3845-3 (proprietary)

These titles were previously published individually by Simon Spotlight with slightly different text and art.

Contents

Meet the Neighbors!

Hi, I'm Daniel Tiger! I live with my mom and dad on Jungle Beach. My friends live all over the neighborhood. They want to meet you! Do you want to meet them too?
Ding, ding!
It's Trolley! Let's go meet the neighbors and find out what they like to do!

This is my friend Katerina Kittycat and her mother, Henrietta Pussycat. They live in a treehouse in the neighborhood.

"Meow, meow," Katerina says. "I like to dance and twirl! Will you be my friend, meow, meow?"

Another friend lives in the tree too. Who, hoo, hoo? It's O the Owl! He loves to read and learn, just like his uncle, X the Owl! "Hoo, hoo!" says O the Owl. "It's true!"

"Books are nifty galifty!" says his uncle.

Did you know there's a castle in the neighborhood? My friend Prince Wednesday lives there with his big brother, Prince Tuesday, and their parents, King Friday and Queen Sara. "A royal hello to you, neighbor!" says Prince Wednesday. "I like being silly. Let's be silly together!"

This is Miss Elaina. She lives in the Museum-Go-Round with her mother, Lady Elaine Fairchilde, and her father, Music Man Stan.

"Welcome to the neighborhood!" says Miss Elaina. "I also like playing pretend . . . and doing things backward!"

There are more neighbors on Main Street. That is where Dr. Anna works in her doctor's office and Baker Aker bakes in his bakery.

"I like helping neighbors feel better," says Dr. Anna.

"And I like baking sweets for them to eat!" says Baker Aker.

Look, Mr. McFeely has a package to deliver! "Speedy Delivery! Speedy Delivery!" he says.
What do you think is inside?

This is my school, and that is Teacher Harriet. She helps my friends and me learn all kinds of things.

"What did you learn today, Daniel?" asks Teacher Harriet.

"I learned that I like my neighborhood—and my friends—more than ever!" I tell her.

Won't you be my neighbor?

Friends Are the Best!

Hi, neighbor! I'm Daniel Tiger. I made a book of pictures of my friend Prince Wednesday and me. Let's look at it together!

This is a picture of Prince Wednesday and me playing toy cars! He didn't have a car, so I shared my tigertastic car with him. Vroom! Vroom!

Friends take turns!

These are pictures of Prince Wednesday and me at a beach . . . an *inside* beach! We wanted to play at an *outside* beach, but it started to rain. We got so mad! Then we helped each other calm down and think of something to do!

Friends help you
when you're mad.

This picture is of Prince Wednesday and me exploring! We're looking for a special gold rock. Can you see it?

Friends explore with you!

Here's a picture from the time I slept over at Prince Wednesday's castle! We saw something scary on the wall, and went together to see what it was. It was only Mr. Lizard's shadow!

Friends help you feel brave.

I am so happy to have a friend like Prince Wednesday . . . and a friend like you! Friends make *everything* better. Ugga Mugga!

How Is Daniel Feeling?

Hi, neighbor. How are you feeling?
I'm feeling happy today with my mom, my dad, and you!
I am smiling to show everyone how happy I am.

But I don't always feel happy. Like that day I wanted to go to the beach and it rained. I felt mad. *Grrr.*

My mom taught me a song:

When you feel so mad that you want to roar, take a deep breath, and count to four.

Counting to four made me feel better. Count to four with me. One. Two. Three. Four.

When I had to go to the doctor to get a shot, I felt scared.

So my mom told me what she does when she feels scared:

Close your eyes and think of something happy.

I thought about riding Trolley through the neighborhood. I didn't feel scared anymore. What happy things can you think about when you're feeling scared?

One day my dad took my friends and me to the Clock Factory. I felt excited! I was so excited that it was hard for me to be calm when I needed to be.

My dad told me what I can do when I need to feel calm:

♪ *Give a squeeze, nice and slow,*
take a deep breath, and let it go.

I felt calm after I did that. Will you take a deep breath with me?

I felt frustrated when I wanted Tigey to sit on top of the block castle but he wouldn't stay.

My mom told me what I could do:

When you're feeling frustrated,
take a step back and ask for help.

I asked my mom to help me rebuild the castle.
We found a way to make Tigey stay on top. I didn't
feel frustrated anymore!

When we took our class pet, Ducky, to the farm, I felt sad. I didn't want Ducky to go.

Teacher Harriet taught me a song:

It's okay to feel sad sometimes.
Little by little, you'll feel better again.

After a while, I did feel a little better. What helps you feel better when you're sad?

Do you know what helps me feel better? Friends, just like Tigey . . . and you! Thank you for being my friend.

Ugga Mugga!

Daniel's Sweet Trip to the Bakery

Hi, neighbor! I'm so glad you're here. We are at Baker Aker's bakery. We are going to surprise my mom and make her some banana bread. It's her favorite treat!

"What ingredients do we need for banana bread?"
Baker Aker asks me.
We need bananas!
"First we peel two bananas, and then we mash them up," says Baker Aker. Mash, mash, mash!

Next my dad
adds the milk . . .

and I get to count
the eggs. One! Two!
My dad cracks the eggs . . .

and Baker Aker adds the
flour. Now it's my turn to
mix everything together.

Mix, mix, mix! Mixing can be messy and so much fun!
Mix, mix, mix!

Now it is time to add three shakes of spicy cinnamon into the bowl. Shake, shake, shake! What else should we add?

"The last ingredient is a little love," says Baker Aker.

Everyone blows a kiss into the room.

Kiss, kiss, kiss!

I pour the mixture into a pan. It's shaped like a heart to show Mom how much we love her! Then Baker Aker puts the pan into the oven. Now we just have to wait for the banana bread to bake.

Waiting is hard, but I know what we can do. We can make believe that the cookies, cakes, and other things in the bakery can sing and dance with us!

Is the banana bread ready yet?
The whole bakery smells *deeeeeelicious*.
Ding! goes the oven. It's ready!

Baker Aker places the banana bread in a box and adds a purple ribbon.
It's perfect! Now my dad and I can take it home.
Thanks, Baker Aker!

Baking with Baker Aker was so much fun! Have you ever made something special for someone? Making something is one way to say "I love you." Thank you for helping me bake today. Ugga Mugga!

Big Brother Daniel

Daniel has some grr-ific news to share. He is a big brother!

"Do you want to meet the baby?" asks Daniel.

"This is my new baby sister, Margaret," Daniel says softly. She is so little.

She cries a lot too.

Daniel says, "Baby Margaret cries so we know that she needs something. And being a big brother means I can help."

You can be a big helper in your family!
Daniel is a big helper. He helps Mom feed the baby.

56

You can be a big helper in your family!
Daniel helps Dad give Baby Margaret a new diaper.

You can be a big helper in your family!
Daniel tells a special story to his baby sister.

Margaret loves her book, *Margaret's Music*. Daniel gave that book to her on the day she was born!

Margaret played piano at the playground, and it sounded like plink, plink, plink!

When Margaret takes a nap, Daniel has some special time with just Mom and Dad. Daniel likes this special time.

Daniel bakes banana bread with Mom and helps
Dad feed the fish.

Daniel says, "Our family is bigger now that Baby Margaret is here. And that makes me happy. You can be a big helper in your family too. Ugga Mugga!"

A Duckling for Daniel

It's springtime in the Neighborhood of Make-Believe, and something very special is happening at school!

"Hi, neighbor!" Daniel Tiger says. "Come with me! I want to show you something exciting!"

In class Teacher Harriet holds up a photo. "Remember when we went to the farm?" she asks.
"That's where we got our duck egg!" Daniel says.
Teacher Harriet says it's almost time for the egg to hatch . . . and for the fuzzy baby duckling that is growing inside to come out!

Daniel and his friends have been waiting a long time for the egg to hatch. Now everyone rushes to peek inside the nest. "Notice anything different today?" asks Teacher Harriet.

Daniel takes a closer look. He sees a crack in the egg!
Miss Elaina gasps when she sees it. "Who broke our egg?"
she asks.

O the Owl tells everyone that the crack in the shell means the baby duck is trying to get out.

Daniel is so excited! "The egg is about to hatch!" he shouts.

But it is not ready yet, so Daniel has to keep waiting.

Daniel is *not* excited about more waiting.
Teacher Harriet knows how to help. "When you wait, you can play, sing, or imagine anything!" she says.

While they wait, Katerina Kittycat twirls . . .

Prince Wednesday plays with blocks . . .

and Daniel imagines he is a duck! "Quack, quack, waddle, waddle!" he says.

Suddenly the egg starts to wiggle and shake.
Daniel's eyes widen with excitement. The egg is finally hatching!

The shell slowly cracks open, piece by piece . . .

. . . and out pops a brand-new, fuzzy yellow duckling!
Everyone oohs and aahs.
After taking a look around, the duckling waddles over to Daniel
and says, "Quack, quack, quack!"
"I think the baby duck just said, 'Hello, neighbor!'" Daniel says.
Daniel is so happy he waited, and waited, and waited for the egg
to hatch . . . because he finally got to meet his new fluffy friend!
"Ugga Mugga!" he says.

You're Still You!

Hi, neighbor! It's me, Daniel Tiger. Do you notice anything different about me? I'm wearing a blue sweater today. I always wear my red sweater, but my mom had to wash it. At first I was worried that if I didn't wear my red sweater, I wouldn't be me. But then my mom made me feel better.

You can change your hair or what you wear, but no matter what you do, you're still you!

I'm still Daniel on the inside, even when I'm wearing a blue sweater.

Prince Wednesday looks different too. He's not wearing his glasses. He always wears his glasses, but today Doctor Anna is fixing them.

You can change your hair or what you wear, but no matter what you do, you're still you!

"Yup! Still me," says Prince Wednesday.

Teacher Harriet has a new hairdo. She usually wears her hair down, but today she has it up in a bun.

You can change your hair or what you wear, but no matter what you do, you're still you!

"Sometimes it's nice to do something different," says Teacher Harriet. "Even though I look different on the outside, I'm still the same Teacher Harriet on the inside."

Prince Wednesday's cousin Chrissie gives me a new hairstyle. I look so different. . . . I don't know if I like it.

"It looks like you have a different hairstyle, Daniel, just like me," says Teacher Harriet. "Do you remember what we said about when you change something on the outside?"

♪ You can change your hair or what you wear, but no matter what you do, you're still you!

I'm still Daniel, no matter what my hair looks like!

Did you ever wear something new or make your hair look different? How did it make you feel? I looked a little different today, but I learned I was still me on the inside. Ugga Mugga!

King Daniel the Kind

King Friday has declared that today Daniel Tiger will be King of the Neighborhood of Make-Believe! Do you see King Daniel's golden crown?

King Daniel says, "I need to do everything on King Friday's royal list, but the most important part about being king is being kind."

 You can choose to be kind!

King Daniel's first stop is the bakery. On his way there, he notices that Prince Tuesday looks hurt. "Prince Tuesday hurt his ankle," says Daniel. "What should I do?"
Daniel remembers:

 You can choose to be kind!

King Daniel finds Dr. Anna and brings her back to Prince Tuesday so she can help him feel better. That is the kind thing to do.

At the bakery, King Daniel gets a sweet treat from Baker Aker to bring to the castle.

A few moments later, Daniel sees O the Owl eating ice cream. "Hi, O!" says Daniel. But as O waves back he drops his ice-cream cone! Oh no! "What can I do?" asks Daniel. Then Daniel remembers:

You can choose to be kind!

King Daniel offers his sweet treat to O, and that makes O so happy! Being kind makes Daniel happy too.

King Daniel's next stop on the list is Music Man Stan's Music Shop to get the loudest instrument, the cymbals!

On his way to the castle to deliver the cymbals, King Daniel notices Miss Elaina. She looks sad.
What can I do to help Miss Elaina? Daniel wonders.
He sings,

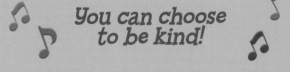

You can choose to be kind!

Daniel offers the cymbals to Miss Elaina. They make her so happy. Being kind makes Daniel feel so good.

King Daniel's last stop is the castle. He doesn't have any of the things King Friday asked for! Daniel is worried he wasn't a good king today.

But then he realizes being king is about helping others and being kind. And Daniel found lots of ways to be kind today.

King Daniel smiles. Being kind made him a good king . . . and a good friend and neighbor.

 *You can choose to be kind!*

Daniel smiles, and he says, "Being kind made me happy. How can you be kind? Ugga Mugga!"

Going to See Grandpere

Hi, neighbor! Guess what? My family and I are going on a trip to visit my Grandpere!
I made something special for him. Do you want to see what it is?

It's a frame with a picture of me and Grandpere! Do you think he'll like it? I'm going to pack it in my backpack right now so I don't forget it.

Ding! Ding! Trolley's here!
To get to Grandpere's house we have to go down the twisty road, past the dinosaur park, and then through the butterfly garden. Mom lets me hold the map.

After the twisty road, we stop at the dinosaur park.
"You can go play on the dinosaur slide," Dad says. We stomp to the slide together like dinosaurs. *Stomp! Stomp! Stomp!*

"Time to get back on Trolley!" Mom calls.
Margaret wants to sit next to me, so we switch seats.
We still have a long way to go, but I can't wait to give Grandpere my picture!

There are so many things to do and see when you're on a trip with your family!
Look at all the butterflies. They're so pretty!
Hey! If this is the butterfly garden, then the next stop on our trip is . . .

. . . Grandpere's house!

"Welcome, my Tiger family!" Grandpere says.

I reach into my backpack to give him my present. He's going to love it!

Wait . . . where *is* my present? Do you see my picture for Grandpere? Dad looks in my backpack. "I don't see it in here, Daniel," Dad says. "We must have lost it along the way."

Oh no! That makes me so sad.

"I know you're sad," Grandpere says. "But maybe there's something else you can give me. You can give me a great big hug!"
There's nothing better than a great big hug!
Even though I lost Grandpere's present, I'm so excited to visit him!
I love being with my family.
Ugga Mugga!

Daniel Loves Fall!

It's a beautiful fall day in the neighborhood!
"Hi, neighbor!" says Daniel Tiger. "Look! Do you see the leaves falling?"
Daniel loves everything about fall, but one of his favorite things is how the leaves are all different colors.
Mom Tiger catches a leaf. "This one's red like your sweater!" she says.

Daniel also loves the Neighborhood Fall Festival, and it's happening tonight! Everyone is busy putting up decorations. "It's going to be *grr-ific!*" Daniel says. "Even Trolley is decorated for fall!"

Daniel's friend Miss Elaina can't wait to show us what her dad, Music Man Stan, is doing for the festival.

"Ta-da!" she says proudly when they get to the music shop. The storefront is covered in all kinds of fall decorations that Music Man Stan made himself!

"Just about done!" says Music Man Stan.

It's beautiful! There are paper leaves around the windows, pinecones painted in fall colors, a scarecrow, a tower of pumpkins stacked one on top of the other, and more. Daniel loves it all. "Look! This pumpkin tower is taller than me!" he says.

All of a sudden, there is a very strong gust of wind. "Whoa. It's so, so, so windy!" Daniel says.
"Oh no! It's blowing everything away!" says Miss Elaina.
They all try to save the decorations, but the wind is too strong, and the decorations are ruined!

"Can you fix them, Dad?" Miss Elaina asks, but Music Man Stan has to teach a piano lesson, so he might not have time.

"Don't you worry about a thing," Mom Tiger says. "We can fix the decorations!"

"Now, that's music to my ears!" says Music Man Stan.

Katerina Kittycat sees what happened and brings new pumpkins to the shop. She and Daniel try to make a new tower like Music Man Stan did, but it keeps falling over.

"How are we going to make a pumpkin tower that's taller than us?" Daniel wonders.

Miss Elaina tries to fix the scarecrow like Music Man Stan did, but it's really hard. "I want its arms to be straight out, the way my dad had them," she says. "But they're too floppy."

"Everyone is different," Mom Tiger tells them. "You don't have to do things the same way. You just need to do your best."
This time they all try to do *their* best instead of Music Man Stan's best. Daniel and Katerina make mini-pumpkin towers, and Miss Elaina arranges the scarecrow's floppy arms into a hug!

Soon the sun sets and the sky turns orange.
It's time for the Fall Festival to start and for Music Man Stan
to see the new decorations.
"Ta-da!" Miss Elaina says proudly.
Music Man Stan is thrilled. "These decorations look better
than ever!" he says.
"We did our best," says Daniel proudly.
And it will be the best Fall Festival yet!

Snowflake Day!

Today is Snowflake Day in the Neighborhood of Make-Believe! Daniel Tiger catches a snowflake on his paw. "Every snowflake is different and special, just like you!" says Daniel's dad.

Daniel and his family walk to the Enchanted Garden for the Snowflake Day celebration. *"It's snowing on Snowflake Day,"* Daniel sings.

All the neighbors have decorated the Enchanted Garden. There are twinkly lights, paper snowflakes, and a big stage for the Snowflake Day show.

Daniel is going to be a snowflake in the show. He puts on his costume and practices what he's going to say onstage.

It's almost time to begin! All of Daniel's friends are working together to make the show sparkle on Snowflake Day!

Making costumes . . .

painting scenery . . .

making food . . .

and making music!

It's time for the show to start. Daniel sees all the people in the audience looking at him.
He feels a little nervous. Maybe he doesn't want to be a snowflake in the show anymore.

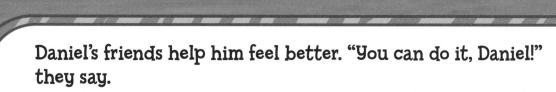

Daniel's friends help him feel better. "You can do it, Daniel!" they say.
Daniel walks back onstage and says his line. "I am a snowflake as special as can be. There is nobody else exactly like me. I'm here to say, let's start the play!"

The Snowflake Day show starts! Daniel and his friends act out the story of a little girl who has lots of presents but is sad because she has no friends. Just when the fairy is about to grant her special wish to have friends . . .

the lights go out in the Enchanted Garden! Oh no! How will they finish the Snowflake Day show in the dark?

Daniel has an idea. They can light up the stage with twinkle lights. Daniel says to the audience, "Twinkle light here, twinkle light there, twinkle lights . . . everywhere!"

The Snowflake Day show is saved! The fairy grants the girl's special wish, and everyone cheers!

Now it's time for everyone to send their twinkle lights up into the snowy sky. Each snowflake is different and special. Just like you. Ugga Mugga!

What's Special at Night?

Hi, neighbor. It's me, Daniel Tiger! My family and I are going for a walk . . . at *night*! You can walk with us!

My dad hands me a flashlight. *Click, click.*
I turn my flashlight on and off and shine it all
around—everything looks so different at night!
What is making that sound? It sounds like
ribbit, ribbit.

Let's find out what's special at night!

It's a frog!
"What other sounds
do you hear?"
my mom asks.

I hear a *tweet, tweet, tweet*. Do you see what's making the noise? Look a little closer with me. It's a nightingale!

Oh, look! Main Street . . . It's so dark! The lights are out at all the shops, but there's still one light on at the bakery.

Let's find out what's special at night!

Baker Aker is baking bread at night. I didn't know he did that!

"He bakes tonight so that he has fresh bread in the morning," my dad explains.

Baker Aker waves to us. Goodnight, Baker Aker!

Over this way, I see Trolley. What's Trolley doing? "Trolley rests at night too," my mom whispers as we walk by.

Look at those tiny lights over there. I wonder what they could be. . . .

Let's find out what's special at night!

133

It's a bunch of fireflies! I use my flashlight to make believe that I'm a firefly too!

My dad laughs. "I bet they've never seen a firefly like you before!"

Oh, wow! Look at all the twinkly stars in the sky. There are so many!

"When I look at the stars, I see pictures," my dad says. "Like those stars over there—they kind of look like a bear. What pictures do you see in the stars?"

Let's find out what's special at night!